Percy the Parrot Yelled Quiet!

Percy the Parrot Yelled Quiet!

By Wayne Carley

Drawings by Art Cumings

GARRARD PUBLISHING COMPANY
CHAMPAIGN. ILLINOIS

Percy the Parrot Yelled Quiet!

Mrs. Gray said,
"I want a pet."

She went
to the pet store.

Mrs. Gray said
to the man,
"I want a pet.
I want a quiet pet."

The man said,
"I have quiet dogs
and quiet cats.
I have a parrot."

Mrs. Gray said,
"I want to see
a quiet dog."

The man said,
"I have
a very quiet dog.
Here she is."

A little dog
was asleep.
She looked very quiet.

The dog
woke up.

The dog barked.
"Yip! Yip! Yip!
Yap! Yap! Yap!
Woof! Woof! Woof!"
The parrot woke up.
"Quiet," said the parrot.

"Quiet," said the man.
"The dog is too noisy,"
said Mrs. Gray.
"Do you have
a quiet cat?"

The man said,
"I have
a very quiet cat.
Here he is."

A big, black cat
was asleep.

The cat woke up.

Quiet

The cat yelled.

"Meow!

Mee-ooo-www!

MEE-OOO-WWWW!"

The parrot woke up.

"Quiet," said the parrot.

"Quiet," said the man.

"The cat is too noisy.
I want a quiet pet,"
said Mrs. Gray.

"This parrot
is very quiet,"
the man said.
"He likes to sleep.
He likes quiet."

The parrot was asleep.

Mrs. Gray woke up
the parrot.
She asked,
"Are you a quiet pet?"

The parrot looked
at Mrs. Gray.
"Quiet," said the parrot.

Mrs. Gray asked,
"Would you like
to be my pet?"
The parrot
was very quiet.

Mrs. Gray said
to the man,
"This parrot
will be a quiet pet.
I will buy him."

Mrs. Gray
took the parrot home.
The parrot
was very quiet.

Mrs. Gray
said to the parrot,
"I don't know
what to call you."

"Percy!"

the parrot said.

Let's have some fun !

"I want a cracker!"
he yelled.
"Turn on the T.V.!"
said Percy.
"Let's have some fun.
It's too quiet here."

"I wanted a quiet pet,"
Mrs. Gray said.
"You are not quiet."
"I'm not quiet,"
said Percy,
"but I'm a lot of fun."

Mrs. Gray laughed.
She said,
"You are fun.
Maybe a noisy pet
will be more fun
than a quiet one."

That's how Percy
became Mrs. Gray's pet.